Oscar Asked, "Why?"

by Jay Hulbert and Sid Kantor

illustrated by Pat Hoggan

METROPOLITAN TEACHING AND LEARNING COMPANY

Copyright ©1999 Metropolitan Teaching and Learning Company. Published by Metropolitan Teaching and Learning Company. All rights reserved. No part of this work may be reproduced or transmitted in any form or by any means electronic or mechanical, including photocopying and recording, or by any information storage or retrieval system without prior written permission of the Metropolitan Teaching and Learning Company unless such copying is expressly permitted under federal copyright law.

Metropolitan Teaching and Learning Company
33 Irving Place
New York, NY 10003

ISBN: 1-58120-972-X

1 2 3 4 5 6 7 8 9 10 CL 05 04 03 02 01 00

Oscar Asked, "Why?"

One Saturday, Oscar asked his mother, "Mami, why is water wet?"

"Good question, Oscar," Papi said.
"But I'm busy, so let's talk later."

Oscar asked his grandmother,
"Nana, why do birds sing?"

"Good question, Oscar," Nana said.
"But I'm busy, so let's talk later."

Oscar asked his brother,
"Ricky, why is a frog green?"

"Good question, Oscar," Mami said.
"But I'm busy, so let's talk later."

Oscar asked his father,
"Papi, why is the sky so high?"

"Good question, Oscar," Ricky said.
"But I'm busy, so let's talk later."

"Why, why, why?" asked Oscar.
"Why doesn't anyone answer my questions?"

Everyone looked at Oscar.

"It's time you got good answers to all your good questions," Papi said.

Then Mami smiled.
"I have an idea," she said.

Mami whispered to Papi. Papi smiled.

Papi whispered to Nana. Nana smiled.
Nana whispered to Ricky. Ricky smiled, too.

"Come on, Oscar," Nana said.
"We're all going to the library."

"Why?" asked Oscar.
"You'll see," Ricky said.

Mami brought Oscar over to meet the librarian.

Soon everyone had books—
books with answers to Oscar's questions.

Oscar smiled. Then he asked his family,

"Why didn't anyone think of this before?"